Hei

HSINAU

# MYSTERY

YOU WRITE IT!

BY JOHN HAMILTON

Published by ABDO Publishing Company, 8000 West 78th Street, Suite 310, Edina, Minnesota 55439.
Copyright ©2009 by Abdo Consulting Group, Inc. International copyrights reserved in all countries.
No part of this book may be reproduced in any form without written permission from the publisher.
ABDO & Daughters™ is a trademark and logo of ABDO Publishing Company.

Printed in the United States.

**Editor:** Sue Hamilton
**Graphic Design:** Sue Hamilton
**Cover Design:** Neil Klinepier
**Cover Illustration:** iStock
**Interior Photos and Illustrations:** p 1 Detective art, Getty Images; p 3 Detective, iStock; p 4 Retro
reporter, iStock; p 5 Monk by Abbey, iStock; p 6 Working on laptop, iStock; p 7 Reader in library,
iStock; p 8 Girl working on laptop, iStock; p 9 Geek with watch, iStock; p 10 *The Hound of the
Baskervilles* DVD, courtesy Mpi Home Video; Basil Rathbone and Nigel Bruce, courtesy 20th
Century Fox; p 11 Index card, iStock; p 12 Detective shoes, iStock; p 13 Peter Sellers as Inspector
Clouseau, Getty Images; p 14 Waiter, iStock; p 15 Nigel Bruce as Dr. Watson, courtesy 20th Century
Fox;  Detective, Comstock; p 16 Man with word balloon, iStock; p 17 Detective interrogates woman,
Getty Images; p 18 Woman working on beach, iStock; Post-it Note, iStock; p 19 Secret agent, iStock;
p 20 Humphrey Bogart and Lauren Bacall in *The Big Sleep*, courtesy Warner Brothers Pictures; p 21
& p 23 Humphrey Bogart in *The Maltese Falcon*, courtesy Warner Brothers Pictures;  p 22 Notebook,
iStock; p 24 Typewriter, iStock; p 25 Man on laptop, iStock; p 26 *Ellery Queen's Mystery Magazine*,
courtesy Dell Magazines; p 27 Man typing, iStock; p 28 *Murder on the Orient Express* book cover,
Berkeley Press; Hercule Poirot, A&E Television Networks; Miss Marple, courtesy Independent
Television; p 29 *A Deadly Game of Magic*, courtesy Harcourt Paperbacks; *Hoot*, courtesy Random
House; *Hoot* movie still, courtesy New Line Cinema; and p 32 Retro reporter, iStock.

Library of Congress Cataloging-in-Publication Data

Hamilton, John, 1959-
  You write it : mystery / John Hamilton.
      p. cm. -- (You write it!)
  Includes index.
  ISBN 978-1-60453-507-5
  1. Detective and mystery stories--Authorship--Juvenile literature.  I. Title.

PN3377.5.D4H36 2009
808.3'872--dc22

                              2008042044

# CONTENTS

# INTRODUCTION

*"Oh dear, I never realized what a terrible lot of explaining one has to do in a murder!"*

—Agatha Christie

The mystery is an extremely popular category of fiction today. There's good reason for this. Most characters in the genre are believable and complex, with enough quirks and hidden motivations to make them very memorable. Some of the most beloved characters of fiction come from the mystery genre: Sherlock Holmes, Miss Marple, Hercule Poirot, … the list goes on and on.

But mysteries contain much more than just memorable characters. Mysteries are mainly plot driven. Unlike a lot of mainstream fiction, they contain strong stories that are propelled by exciting events that leap across the page. Many mysteries are "whodunits," delightful puzzles that readers love trying to solve. Mysteries also explore the dark side of human nature, wrestling with fascinating subjects such as murder, violence, and justice.

Thousands of mystery books, short stories, movies, and TV shows are created each year. Perhaps you've got a mystery story *you're* dying to tell. But where to start?

Novelist Gene Fowler once said, "Writing is easy. All you do is stare at a blank sheet of paper until drops of blood form on your forehead." What he meant is that writing is much harder than it looks. Anybody who can form a simple sentence thinks they can write. But good writing, like any other skill, takes practice.

Few people are born writers. But there are certain skills anyone can learn. These "tools of the trade" can help you master the craft of writing. And once you've mastered the *craft,* you're well on your way to writing mystery stories that others will love. You will encounter many obstacles along the way, but good writers find a way. The important thing is persistence, and a burning desire to tell your story.

## Setting

A mystery's setting is very important. A spooky house, dark woods, a bad neighborhood... a believable, well-designed setting almost becomes one of the characters. Be sure not to limit yourself; a mystery can take place almost

anywhere. In Umberto Eco's *The Name of the Rose*, the hero was a Franciscan friar, and the setting was a murder-filled medieval abbey. Mystery settings are limited only by your imagination.

*Left:* A mystery story's setting is important. It can be a spooky house or even a medieval abbey.

# IDEAS

*"The secret of getting ahead is getting started."*

—Agatha Christie

The number one question asked of professional writers is, where do you get your ideas? It's usually asked by insecure beginners who are afraid they don't have the imagination it takes to be successful. But as you'll soon find out, ideas are everywhere: in your head, in the morning newspaper, in a stray conversation overheard at the bus stop. Developing an idea into a *story* is where the hard work takes place.

Local newspapers are a wealth of idea-generating stories. Read the community/crime section. Twist a story and make the emotions and passions even stronger. Say a man filed a police complaint against a neighbor who held noisy backyard parties. What if the police did nothing? How far would the man go to stop the parties? Would he resort to blackmail? Even murder?

**Popular Mystery Categories**
Private Eye—Citizens who solve crimes, either as licensed investigators or as amateur sleuths.
Police Procedural—Professional law-enforcement officers
Heists and Capers—Criminal masterminds who plan and carry out elaborate, high-stakes thefts.

# Coming Up With Ideas

- You must *read* in order to write. This is especially true with mystery fiction. Read a lot. Every day.
- Write what you know! Use your past experiences, then translate them into ideas.
- Brainstorm! Time yourself for two minutes. Jot down any ideas that pop into your head. Don't edit yourself, even if you think the ideas are stupid. They may spark even more creativity later.
- Keep a daily journal. It can be a diary or a blog, but it can also include ideas that pop into your head, drawings, articles, photos, etc. As you accumulate information, you'll see patterns begin to emerge of things that interest you the most. Explore these themes.
- Read crime journals, magazines, and web sites. What interests you the most? How can you take a story from today's headlines and make it even more dramatic?
- Write down your dreams. And your daydreams.

*Right:* If you want to be a writer, be a reader. Read everything from newspapers to magazines to mystery books. Then write down your ideas.

# WORK HABITS

*"Work every day. No matter what has happened the day or night before, get up and bite on the nail."*

—Ernest Hemingway

Established writers will tell you over and over, the only way to learn to write is to write every day. It bears repeating: write… every… day. You wouldn't hire a carpenter to build your house unless he or she had a lot of practice in the craft, right? Do you think Michael Phelps broke swimming speed records the first time he jumped in a pool? Of course not! He spent thousands of hours in the water refining and perfecting his technique before he won his first gold medal. Writing is like any other craft or sport: it takes practice.

Find your own special place to write, a place where you can work uninterrupted. You can't wait for the mood to strike. You have to make time, even if you're busy. J.K. Rowling famously wrote much of *Harry Potter and the Sorcerer's Stone* in neighborhood cafes. (Her baby fell asleep during walks, so she ducked into cafes to take advantage of precious writing time.) If you have a laptop, you might think you can write anywhere. But it's usually best to find a single place to write. A desk in your bedroom might do, especially if you can close the door.

Or maybe a corner table in the library, or a quiet nook in a coffee shop. Think of it as your home base. Psychologically, it will help you tune out the world and get down to the business of writing.

Friends and family can be a terrible distraction. Even a minor interruption can stall your creativity. Enlist their help by making clear to them that you need to be left alone during your writing time. It doesn't always work, of course. But as you become a more practiced writer, it will take you less and less time to recover from life's inevitable distractions.

## Don't Plagiarize

Writers are creative people. They want to bring their own ideas to life and share them with the world. Sometimes, though, deadline pressure (or sheer laziness) causes people to plagiarize others' work. Stealing somebody else's writing is a terrible idea. Not only is it totally wrong, it can bring you serious trouble. You can be suspended from school, expelled from college, or fired from a job. Don't do it! Besides, the world wants to read what springs from *your* mind, not somebody else's.

*Right:* Never steal somebody else's writing, even when under deadline pressure. Always write your own ideas.

# CHARACTER CREATION

*"First, find out what your hero wants, then just follow him!"*
—Ray Bradbury

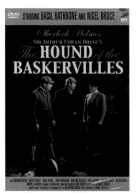

What's more important, plot or character? Some writers say plot. After all, your readers are expecting a good story. On the other hand, think of the best books you've ever read. Chances are, what you remember most are the interesting characters. What would *The Hound of the Baskervilles* be without Sherlock Holmes and Dr. Watson?

The truth is, both elements are critical to good storytelling. You can't have one without the other. The reason characters are so memorable is because they are the key to unlocking the emotions of your story. You empathize with them, feel what they feel. Through great characters, you have an emotional stake in the outcome of the story. If you don't care about the characters, why should you care how the story turns out?

*Right:* Great characters, such as Sherlock Holmes and Dr. Watson, make for a great plot.

# Character Biographies

Good writers are people watchers. Study the people you meet every day. Start a character journal; write down what makes these people interesting to you. Observe their physical characteristics and their behavior. What quirks do they have? How do they dress? How do they walk and talk? Mold and twist these traits into your own fictional characters.

Many writers find it helpful to create very detailed biographies of all their major characters. This sometimes helps you to discover your characters' strengths and weaknesses, which you can use later when you throw them into the boiling stew of your plot.

Backstory is the history you create for your characters. Most of it may never make it into your final draft, but it helps make your characters seem more "real" as you write.

# Character Biography Checklist

Below is a list of traits you might want to consider for each of your characters. You should at least know this backstory information for your hero and main villain. What other traits can you think of that will round out your characters' biographies?

## Character Biography Checklist

- ✓ Character's full name
- ✓ Nickname
- ✓ Age/Birthdate
- ✓ Color of eyes/hair
- ✓ Height/weight
- ✓ Ethnic background
- ✓ Physical imperfections
- ✓ Glasses/contacts
- ✓ Family background
- ✓ Spouse/children
- ✓ Religion
- ✓ Politics
- ✓ School
- ✓ Special skills
- ✓ Military
- ✓ Job/profession
- ✓ Hobbies/sports
- ✓ Bad habits
- ✓ Fears
- ✓ Hopes and dreams

# Character is Action

Characters are revealed through their actions. Instead of telling us that your detective is smart, show him completing a crossword puzzle in record time, or correctly deducing the hometown of a suspected criminal by observing the bottom of the man's shoe. Okay, that's a little bit extreme, and cliché, but you get the idea. The point is, it's always better to reveal your characters' personalities through their behavior. Let their actions speak for themselves. It's one of the basic rules of fiction: show, don't tell!

# Viewpoint

Whose "voice" is telling your story? The vast majority of fiction uses one of two viewpoints: first person and third person. First-person viewpoint uses the "I" voice, as if the reader were experiencing the action personally. (*"I hurried down the dark alley, my hand nervously gripping the pistol in my pocket."*) First-person can be used very effectively to inhabit the thoughts and feelings of your main character. For mysteries, an added bonus is that in first person, your reader knows only what your main character knows. This makes solving the story's puzzle even more fun.

On the other hand, third-person viewpoint (often called "third-person omniscient," or "the eye of God") lets you describe things your main character might not be aware of. You can describe your characters' feelings, but you can also take a step back and view the action from a more distant, neutral viewpoint. (*"Detective Smith moved nervously through the dark alley, the sound of his footsteps echoing off the wet brick walls of the abandoned buildings. Up ahead, hidden in the shadows, a thug waited patiently."*) For beginning writers, third-person viewpoint is a good choice. It has fewer pitfalls and complications.

Short stories almost always use a single viewpoint throughout. In longer forms, like novels, some authors like to mix up viewpoints for variety. Varying viewpoints can be very entertaining, but remember to keep the same viewpoint in each scene. Otherwise, you'll confuse your reader.

# Heroes

Your hero is your main character, or protagonist. He or she is the person the story is about. It's through the hero that your readers experience your story, and make an emotional connection with the other characters.

In mysteries, heroes come in many flavors: private eyes, amateur sleuths, police professionals. Some are hard-boiled and tough, while others rely on their intellect to solve crimes. As a writer, keep in mind the one thing all these heroes should have in common: they should be likable. Mystery readers will quickly abandon your book if your hero is disagreeable.

To make your hero likeable, make him a capable person. He should be competent enough to solve the crime on his own, without calling in the cavalry. Give him a likeable trait or two. And be sure to give him a personal stake in the story. The reader will be much more engaged if the hero is personally threatened by the villain in some way. This is why in fiction so many villains kidnap or threaten the hero's family members. As a story device, it gives the hero a direct stake in the outcome of the story.

Also, don't forget to give your heroes some flaws to overcome. This makes them seem more human, and interesting. Readers will root for heroes if they can relate to their fears and insecurities.

*Left:* One of the most endearing detectives is Inspector Jacques Clouseau (played by Peter Sellers) in the *Pink Panther* films.

Create a villain who is likeable, and you've created a special character.

# The Villain

The villain is the antagonist of the story, the one who tries to keep your hero from accomplishing his or her goal. Villains can be great fun to write. Many villains in mysteries are pure evil, but the most effective ones have weaknesses and motivations we can relate to. Nobody's afraid of a villain who's all bluster and anger. But create a villain who seems like someone we could bump into on the street, and you've created something special.

An effective technique is to make your villains charming. It's what the villains use to lure their innocent victims, including your readers. It makes them villains we love to hate. In mystery stories, it confuses and misleads the reader. Could the polite, hard-working butler really be a killer?

One thing you must know in a mystery is this: what motivates your villain? Why is he angry enough to rob a bank, or commit murder? Show why the villain behaves the way he does. Perhaps he was beaten as a child, or feels he is righting some sort of injustice. If you can humanize your villain in this way, the reader will become more emotionally involved in your story.

# Secondary Characters

Secondary characters are critical to how your hero overcomes the problems you throw his way. Many types of secondary characters show up again and again in stories. Joseph Campbell, the great scholar of mythology, identified many characters who have common purposes. He called them archetypes, a kind of common personality trait first identified by psychologist Carl Jung.

A *mentor*, or "wise old man or woman," gives critical help or knowledge to the hero. In a mystery, he might take the form of a sidekick. Sherlock Holmes's friend Dr. Watson is probably the most famous sidekick in mystery fiction. One big advantage of a sidekick is that it lets the author bounce ideas around in the form of dialogue between the two characters, which is almost always more interesting than straight narration. Informers are also another kind of mentor.

*Threshold guardians* are characters who block the hero along the way. Threshold guardians test the hero, preparing him to battle the main villain later in the story.

*Tricksters* are helper characters who can be mischievous even as they assist the hero. Sometimes these characters are sidekicks who provide comic relief in contrast to the serious hero. A story that is serious all the time can be exhausting to read. Tricksters can help lighten the mood between dramatic scenes.

How will you create and use your secondary characters? You might want to create character biographies the way you did with your hero and villain. You should at least know what motivates them. How are they critical to the story, and why do they act the way they do?

# Dialogue

Good dialogue propels the story. If you simply restate the obvious, then your dialogue is too "on the nose." After describing a man being shot during the course of a robbery, you probably don't need him to say to your hero, "I've been shot!" Instead, have him say something that also reveals his character, like, "Tell my wife I love her." Or maybe something unexpected, like, "Please take care of my dog." In addition to giving information, good dialogue adds mood and suspense.

When writing dialogue speech verbs, a simple "he said" or "she said" is best. Too many beginning writers clutter their dialogue with unnecessary adverbs in order to show a character's emotions: *"Tell me why you threw her over the bridge," the detective said angrily.* So, what's so bad about "angrily"? It's much better to *show* action instead of using an adverb.

*Above:* When writing dialogue speech, a simple "he said" or "she said" is best. Adverbs can be used for variety.

Remember, character is action. Show, don't tell! For example: *The detective slowly set down his glass of water, then stared hard at the nervous man sitting across the table. "Tell me why you threw her over the bridge," he said.*

For a different mood, show a different action: *The detective opened the file, uncapped his pen, then crisply put the point to the first line on the paper. "Tell me why you threw her over the bridge," he said.* Two different reactions, but in each case the writer simply used "he said."

Start a dialogue notebook. Write down speech you overhear at home, during lunch hour, or at the mall. You'll quickly discover that real speech is very different from written dialogue. Real speech often overlaps, and is filled with "ums," "ers," and "likes." Written dialogue should not mimic real speech; real speech on the page quickly becomes tedious.

Write down interesting figures of speech you overhear. Idioms like "he threw me a curve" or "kick the bucket" can be great for creating interesting characters. But be sparing when writing regional dialects. A little goes a long ways.

*Above:* Good dialogue propels a story forward. Pay attention to how people speak in real life to get an idea how to write appropriate dialogue.

# PLOTS

*"Fiction is a lie, and good fiction is the truth inside the lie."*
—Stephen King

Planning a piece of fiction, especially a long piece like a novel, can be a daunting task. It becomes more manageable if you break it down into smaller parts. You've probably already learned in school that fiction has three key elements: a beginning, middle, and an end. That seems simple enough. These are sometimes referred to as Acts I, II, and III. Acts I and III (the beginning and end) are critical pieces of the story, but are relatively short. Act II holds the guts of the story, where the majority of the action takes place.

The beginning of a story is called the "hook." How do you best capture your readers' interest? Many authors, surprisingly, don't start at the beginning. Instead, their books start with a bang, right in the middle of the action, with the hero embroiled in an exciting scene. Only after the scene's action is resolved do we take a step back and reveal the major characters and setting. Remember, character is action. By starting with an action scene, we automatically learn something about the main character.

Three Key Elements of Fiction
Act I - Beginning—Introduction
Act II - Middle—Rising Action
Act III - End—Falling Action/Resolution

## To Outline or Not?

Many writers create outlines of their story, right down to a scene-by-scene description of the action and each character's part in it. Sometimes they use notecards, which can be shuffled around until all the scenes are arranged just right.

Other authors shun outlines. They start with an idea, add a strong character or two, and then let their storytelling sense guide them along the way. These authors argue that rigid outlines stifle creativity.

So, who's right? They both are. Great works of fiction have been written using both methods. But be warned that people who don't use outlines usually have to go back and do much more editing and revising after their first drafts are finished. Outlines provide a nice roadmap for beginning writers. Don't think

of an outline as a rigid pathway; you can make changes along the way, and you probably will. But at least you've got a guide to help steer your story toward a satisfying conclusion.

## Hero's Journey

After the beginning, how do you establish the plot and tie it all together? In *The Hero With a Thousand Faces,* author Joseph Campbell described patterns that are common to almost all works of fiction. They form a structure that authors use to tell the same basic tale, a story about a hero who goes on a quest to find a prize and bring it back to his or her tribe.

Some writers think it's useful to keep this "hero's journey" in mind as they dream up their own stories. Of course, you don't have to rigidly follow the structure. It is merely a guide. But if you really study the books and movies you enjoy, you'll discover many of the following elements hidden within.

# Act I

## The Ordinary World

This section introduces the hero before the adventure begins. Typical mysteries show a private eye in his or her office, or a policeman reporting for duty at the precinct. What does your hero want? What's at stake?

## The Call to Adventure

This is where some sort of event happens that gets the story moving. There may be a message or temptation that calls your hero to act. The message is often delivered by a type of character, or archetype, called a herald. In many private-eye stories, a mysterious client brings a puzzling case to the hero.

## Crossing the Threshold

This is the point where the hero makes a decision (or a decision is made for him), and he's thrown into the adventure. A critical event called a plot point occurs.

*Above:* Actor Humphrey Bogart often played the classic tough private eye. Lauren Bacall was frequently cast as his mysterious client.

## Engage Your Senses

Russian novelist Anton Chekhov once said, "Don't tell me the moon is shining; show me the glint of light on broken glass." Use all your senses. Is there a hint of sweetness to the air, or is it stale? What sound does the wind make when it blows through a darkened alley? Show, don't tell.

## Act II

## Tests and Conflict

Act II is for testing the hero. What allies does she meet? What enemies? Who is the chief villain, and what are his goals? Does our hero act alone, or does she gather a group together, a posse?

Act II is a series of rising actions and mini-climaxes. In real life, events happen in seemingly random order. But in a good story, each event the hero encounters is connected, leading to the next ordeal.

## The Crisis

The crisis is a point in the story where the hero faces her most fearsome test yet, perhaps even enduring a brush with death. It's the "dragging the hero through the gutter" scene, where the hero's faith in himself is put to the ultimate test. Then the hero makes a realization, or figures out a puzzle, and sets off for the final conflict.

# Act III

## The Final Struggle

This is the point in the story where the hero uses everything he's learned and faces the ultimate test. In many mystery stories, the conflict becomes a physical action; the final struggle is a fight of some kind.

## Deus Ex Machina

It's always best if your character wins the conflict on his own, especially if he uses skills learned during the course of the story. Beware of having another character swoop in to save the day. This kind of ending is called a *deus ex machina,* a Latin phrase that means "machine of the gods." In some ancient Greek plays, a cage with an actor portraying a god inside was lowered onto the stage, where he would miraculously solve the hero's seemingly hopeless problems. You've probably read books or watched movies where a similar event happened: an unexpected person or situation arises and saves the day. This is what some critics refer to as a contrived ending. Don't resort to this! You've spent the whole story building up your hero with new wisdom and skills. Let him save himself. Otherwise, what's the point of telling your story?

**How To Build Suspense:**

- Add a "ticking clock," a deadline that must be met.

- Keep the action moving.

- Give each suspect a motive for committing the crime.

- Introduce red herrings—false clues that misdirect the reader.

- Use cliffhangers at the end of chapters.

# The Return

In many stories, the hero finally returns to his normal world. He brings back a prize, a symbolic magical elixir that benefits his people. Maybe it's gold, or medicine, or simply wisdom. But whatever the prize, what really matters is how the hero has changed (or didn't change) during his epic journey.

*Above:* In *The Maltese Falcon,* Humphrey Bogart gazes at the elusive prize.

# REWRITING

*"It is perfectly okay to write garbage—as long as you edit brilliantly."*

—C.J. Cherryh

So, you finally finished your story. Congratulations! Whether it's a short story or a novel, you've achieved something most people only dream of. Take a step back, celebrate a little, and then get ready for more work, because there's a truth that you will soon discover: writing is rewriting. Editing your work is a crucial part of the entire process.

Don't edit yourself until you've cranked all the way through your story. If you edit while you write, you'll find things you don't like. It will stifle your creativity as you struggle to make things "perfect." Get that first draft finished, then go back and edit.

First, set your story aside for a couple weeks, or at least a few days. Amazingly, with fresh eyes you'll catch mistakes that snuck under your radar the first time around. Your second draft will be better than your first. Your third draft will be an even bigger improvement. Edit and polish your story until it shines. How many drafts do you need? It depends on the story. Some authors do a dozen drafts, others are content with only one or two drafts of editing after the first. You're done when you know in your heart that you've written your story to the very best of your ability.

If you're a writer, then you know the importance of good grammar and spelling. There's no substitute for carefully proofing the story with your own two eyes.

Examine your plot. Are the characters well formed? Do they grow and change? Most important, is your hero likeable? Does the hero have traits we admire? Can we identify with him or her? Do we care if the hero succeeds?

What about the beginning of your book? Does it grab the reader by the throat and never let go?

Are there scenes or events that are really necessary to push the story forward? Be honest with yourself. Be ruthless. Your story will be stronger the tighter you make it. Always, always remember your readers.

Keep your paragraphs short.

When appropriate, use active verbs instead of passive verbs. Instead of "Officer Smith was shot by the bank robber," try "The banker robber shot Officer Smith." See how much more immediate and interesting that simple change made the sentence?

Make sure you keep one point of view per scene.

Read your dialogue out loud. Does it sound natural? Does each character have his or her own "voice"?

# GET PUBLISHED

*"The reason 99 percent of all stories written are not bought by editors is very simple. Editors never buy manuscripts that are left on the closet shelf at home."*

—John Campbell

Your story is written and edited—now what? There are many web sites that publish work by young writers. Do an Internet search for "mystery webzines" to find good sites. Many of these web sites are also terrific places to learn your craft, with free advice from established authors. You won't get paid much (if anything), but it's a way to get your work seen by an enthusiastic audience.

Or, you could start your own web site and publish online yourself. Some authors post the first chapter or two of their books as a free download, then charge a small fee if the reader wants more. Other authors post their entire work online, happy just to receive reader feedback.

## Other Options:

- School newspapers or yearbooks. These publications are always hungry for material.
- Local, regional, or national creative-writing contests.
- Creative-writing clubs and workshops. These are a great way to get feedback from other writers. They also give you practice in critiquing others' work, which will improve your own writing.

- Local newspapers and magazines are always looking for new talent, especially if they can get it for cheap. Still, you have to start somewhere, and it's a way to get your work read by a large audience.
- Self publish. With today's page-layout software, it's easier than ever to create your own publication. Make copies for friends and family.

## Publishers

If you are determined to have your story accepted by an established book publisher, first make sure your manuscript is ready. A clean, typewritten, double-spaced, mistake-free manuscript will go a long way in making your story stand out from all the rest. There are many "writer's guide" publications, some available at your library, you can use to research mystery markets. They can also tell you how to write a query letter. Put your manuscript in a self-addressed stamped envelope (SASE), wish yourself luck, and mail it off. But please don't sit around waiting for a reply. Keep reading and writing!

## Final Thoughts

If you receive a rejection letter, don't despair. Everybody gets them! Remember, the publisher isn't rejecting you, only your story. Maybe your writing isn't strong enough just yet. Or maybe your writing is fine, but the publisher isn't buying stories like yours at this time. Trends come and go in the marketplace, but don't try to write what you think publishers are looking for. By the time you finish your book, the fickle public will have moved on to the Next Big Thing. Simply write what you love, and the rest will follow.

You have the gift of storytelling. Sometimes you just need good timing and a little bit of luck. But remember, the more persistent you are, the luckier you'll get. Keep writing!

# ADVICE FROM MYSTERY WRITERS

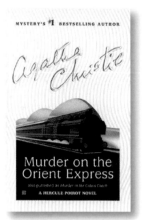

*"Crime is terribly revealing. Try and vary your methods as you will, your tastes, your habits, your attitude of mind, and your soul is revealed by your actions."*

*"The best time to plan a book is while you're doing the dishes."*

## Agatha Christie (1890-1976)

Agatha Christie was a best-selling English mystery writer who penned 80 detective novels, plus many short stories and plays. Her fictional detectives, including Hercule Poirot and Miss Jane Marple, are some of the most beloved characters in the mystery genre. Dubbed the "Queen of Crime," Christie's novels have sold about 4 billion copies, second only to the Bible in sales. Her most popular works include *Murder on the Orient Express, And Then There Were None,* and *Death on the Nile.*

*Left:* Hercule Poirot and Miss Jane Marple are two of Agatha Christie's most popular characters.

*"A mystery begins to develop in my mind when something sparks an idea and a question grows from it. What would it be like to move into a house in which a murder had taken place? How would I feel if my best friend were arrested for murder on circumstantial evidence? ... Before I write a word of the story I know how I'll begin it and how I'll end it, making sure to put in honest clues and distracting red herrings—just to make the mystery all the more fun to solve."*

# Joan Lowery Nixon (1927-2003)

Joan Lowery Nixon was a journalist and author who wrote many award-winning mysteries for young adults and children. She especially enjoyed creating lead characters that were strong, young women who could think their way out of difficult situations. She wrote more than 140 books, and won four Edgar Allan Poe Awards from the Mystery Writers of America.

*"When I begin a novel, I've got a premise and a cast of characters and that's about all. I don't do outlines because they inherently limit the plot possibilities. I want the freedom to change directions if needed, and I want to be surprised by my characters. Those are the great joys of writing novels. If I wanted to know in advance how my books were to end, I'd write nonfiction instead."*

# Carl Hiaasen (1953- )

Carl Hiaasen is an American journalist and mystery writer. His comic thrillers usually take place in his home state of Florida, which he depicts as a hotbed of greedy

businessmen and crooked politicians. His first novel for young adults, *Hoot,* won a Newbery Honor Award. It's the story of three friends who try to stop a construction project that threatens a group of burrowing owls.

# HELPFUL READING

- *Writing Mysteries* edited by Sue Grafton

- *You Can Write a Mystery* by Gillian Roberts

- *Writing the Modern Mystery* by Barbara Norville

- *Mystery Writer's Handbook* edited by Lawrence Treat

- *The Writer's Journey: Mythic Structure for Writers* by Christopher Vogler

- *The Hero With a Thousand Faces* by Joseph Campbell

- *Stein on Writing* by Sol Stein

- *Self-Editing for Fiction Writers* by Renni Browne and Dave King

- *Writing Dialogue* by Tom Chiarella

- *Building Believable Characters* by Marc McCutcheon

- *Zen in the Art of Writing* by Ray Bradbury

- *The Elements of Style* by William Strunk, Jr., and E.B. White

- *The Transitive Vampire* by Karen Elizabeth Gordon

- *Roget's Super Thesaurus* by Marc McCutcheon

- *2009 Writer's Market* by Robert Brewer

- *Jeff Herman's Guide to Publishers, Editors, & Literary Agents 2009* by Jeff Herman

# GLOSSARY

**Antagonist** — Often called the villain, the antagonist is an important character who tries to keep the hero from accomplishing his or her goal.

**Archetype** — A type of character that often appears in stories. Archetypes have special functions that move the story along, such as providing the hero with needed equipment or knowledge.

**Backstory** — The background and history of a story's characters and setting. When writing, it is good to know as much backstory as possible, even if most of it never appears in the final manuscript.

**Cliffhanger** — The ending of a scene or chapter that has unfinished action, leaving the audience in suspense.

**First-Person Viewpoint** — The "I" viewpoint, which makes it seem as if the person telling the story is the one who experienced it first-hand. "I grabbed my gun and turned to meet the gangsters," is an example of first-person viewpoint.

**Genre** — A type, or kind, of a work of art. In literature, a genre is distinguished by a common subject, theme, or style. Some genres include science fiction, fantasy, mystery, and horror.

**Hook** — The beginning of a story, used to grab a reader's interest.

**Plagiarism** — To copy somebody else's work.

**Point of View** — The eyes, or viewpoint, through which we experience a story or scene.

**Protagonist** — A story's hero or main character. The protagonist propels the story.

**Red Herring** — A false clue that is intended to mislead the reader, to distract from the real solution to the crime.

**Third-Person Viewpoint** — A detached, neutral point of view in which the story is told by an all-seeing narrator. "Detective Smith moved nervously through the dark alley," is an example of third-person viewpoint.

# INDEX